The Lives of Atoms

Lee Okan

Nixes Mate Books
Allston, Massachusetts

Copyright © 2018 Lee Okan

Book design by d'Entremont
Cover photograph by Lauren Leja

Every writer is indebted to another. I had the luck to be tutored by William Melvin Kelley at Sarah Lawrence College. Willy taught me to master my voice. I then had the fortune to study with Tony Eprile at Lesley University. Tony taught me discipline. I want to thank Willy and Tony for training me as a writer. I want to thank my publisher, Nixes Mate and Michael McInnis, for guiding *The Lives of Atoms* into the world. Lastly, I want to thank the man who I love, my first reader, Melih Okan.

ISBN 978-0-9993971-6-9

Nixes Mate
POBox 1179
Allston, MA 02134

To Melih, hayatım.

Hayatıma küçük bir aşk mektubu

The Lives of Atoms

"Tell me a story," she said. The scientist's wife turned
her face towards his. They lay in bed in the darkness as
car lights flickered off their walls. The sudden roar of a
commuter train rushed below their window. When its
clamor dissolved into the night, the tremor of the rails
quieting, they folded in together against the tumult
outside their windows, their world, and the scientist
smelled the sweet breath of his wife as she repeated,
"Tell me a story."

"What kind of story?" Aslan asked her, kissing her hairline. Her face was in the well of his chest, a hand draped over his side. She was his beauty, she was his. He kissed her hairline again as she paused below his chin. Manu exhaled and all her sweetness, of flowers and the dinner she ate with her pink lips. She sighed and told her husband, "Tell me the story about atoms."

Aslan brushed her hair back away from his lips and cajoled her; surely she did not want to hear about atoms, the data screens, the numbers he analyzed all day. He was not very good at telling stories at all, darling, why do you want me to tell a story at all, at all about atoms?

"Because," she answered with a feline yawn and pressed closer to his body, "Because you talk about atoms as if they were people, too. Tell me what they did today."

He had studied physics for so long, the subject was sewn into the fabric of his life. He could not detach it from one holiday or another summer, and it always was, always breathing in the background of his life as the seasons fell and the seasons fell. And he had studied atoms for so long, he stuttered once or twice to tell the story, pulling in different directions, until beginning with the universe and bosons, but changed his mind mid-sentence and told her the story of entangled atoms.

Sometimes, the scientist began, seemingly independent particles become intertwined. For example, let's say that there is an atom in Turkey, he said touching her thigh with his finger, while in Cambridge, and he kissed her face, there is another atom. Even though the atoms may be far apart, they are no longer independent of each other. When one is touched, he said, touching her thigh, the other reacts, he said, touching her face.

One particle knows what measurement has been performed on the other, and with what outcome, though separated by long distances.

Our particle in Cambridge, asleep in bed after a shower and a long day, drifting off to sleep feels a sudden tickle on her thigh. And so Aslan tickled her thigh. Our other particle in Turkey, yearning to return home, waiting in the airport after delays and deluge of administration, feels a sudden tickle on his thigh. Each suddenly knows what the other felt, despite distance, despite time.

Aslan liked to lounge in bed as long as he could in the mornings, waiting until it was too late, he was too late, but he hardly ever rushed anywhere. Manu was already gone. He rolled onto his side and held her absent form. Her scent lingered in the pillow. In the early morning, like a dream he remembered her body rise and a brush of kisses across his face and eyes and chin. She caressed his hair each time he tried to open his eyes, whispering, Sleep my love, go back to sleep, and he did so easily, her hand running through his hair, falling asleep as her lips glimmered across his ear, I love you.

His wife had already biked across the city with her elegant long legs made golden by the summer light, already sitting through the first meeting of the day, her pen to the corner of her bottom lip, frowning as she did when she tended to disagree. He was merely waking now, pulling past the comforter to use the bathroom.

In an hour, after dawdling at the computer for the day's news, Aslan took the elevator to the first floor and walked to work. He carried nothing, except for his wallet, because he did not like the burden of things. As he walked across the bridge that cut over the commuter rail tracks, he realized he had forgotten his sunglasses and returned once more to retrieve them.

A second time, Aslan set off for work, his eyes now relieved by the heavy June sun. All around him, others were still setting off for work, women in light, wafting dresses, men carrying their bags splayed across their shoulders. As he waited to cross the intersection, he looked up towards the sun, and lowered his gaze. Ah, there, it had gone behind a building, and he walked freely from the brightness.

He saw a dark figure crouched on the edge of the sidewalk, and looked again, no, only a trashcan, and he heard the garbage trucks rolling down the street then, stopping and loud beeping, as the men collected first one bin, then another, shouting, whistling, tossing the bin back on the street. Optical misfire, he shook his head.

As he crossed down another street, with a casual glance he took in his reflection. He caught the eyes of a woman looking at him, too, and another passing by, a quick look before she crossed the street. He noticed sometimes women looking at him as he passed, some-times the students. He told Manu of the attention once, and she said distractedly, "Well, yes, of course…" and returned to writing. But he caught her looking at him, too, on the way from the bathroom, sometimes while they were eating. He liked her tender looks, but could never know what she was really thinking, "What?" "I love you."

He stopped at a cafe before going to the lab because he was hungry and had not eaten yet. By the time he arrived at the lab, it was close to noon, and he was hot from the walk over. He rested and began his research.

Aslan, the scientist worked in a lab for hours at a time, pushing a button and collecting data. He cooled the atoms and contained them into a box and tried to predict where they would go. They were as unmanageable as humanity, moving towards some distant unknown.

He pushed the button, collected data. Around early evening, he took a break and had dinner with friends at a nearby restaurant. Perhaps humanity was more predictable, he thought, biting into a sandwich he always ordered from the restaurant they always went.

Aslan stayed later than he intended to, wanted to, knowing his wife was already home. She had asked him, "What do you want for dinner?" He was dismayed, knowing she would be asleep by the time he returned.

Manu lingered in and out of his mind as he worked. He thought of the first time he had brought her to the lab, watched her eyes move over the heavy machinery, the colored light of the lasers. "These are atoms?" she asked, peering into the microscope. Aslan watched her push her hair out of her face, look up at him and smile.

"Tell me," she said, "What are you trying to do?"

I work with ultra cold gases, the scientist said, at temperatures a million times colder than interstellar space and at densities a million times thinner than air. When the gases are near absolute zero, atoms begin to behave as waves and interfere like laser lights. They begin to form new states of matter. In these ultra cold temperatures, atoms join together as pairs that flow without friction.

And I observe them. I cool them down with my different colored lasers; I capture them in cages of light. I study them and take photos of them. I forecast and try to understand how and why they move as they do. It is hard to ever really know them entirely. I let them loose, out of their cages of colored lights. They disappear into the mass of other atoms. They never miss me, I'm sure.

What can we hope to learn from all of this? We want to use these gases as model systems, the study of neutron stars.

If you look, there, between all the machinery, do you see the atoms? The glowing yellow light. Yes, they do

not look like much at all to our untooled eyes. A mass
of something unfamiliar. And yet we can see it all with
our eyes, the scientist said, looking at his girlfriend,
looking – and he knew – at his eternal love, It is a
remarkable thing, isn't it?

In August they went to the sea. Manu liked to sail and
so set out on a little dinghy while Aslan waited on the
shore flipping through a magazine. He could see her
white sail growing smaller and smaller as she moved
quickly out, and when she was only a speck on the
horizon, he grew impatient, no longer looked through
the readings, but waited with eyes scanning above the
pages, searching the horizon for his wife.

He dug his hand into the sand, enjoying the coolness
as he touched below the surface, deeper and deeper
until it was pleasant and cool. He did the same with his
feet, hiding the tops from the burn of the sun. And he
waited. His eyes drifted from the sea, the waves spray-
ing on the shore, to the sand around him, and noted
with fascination, the insects scurrying between the
grains of sand. Every now and again, too, the sand gave
away into a pit as if suggesting a creature below was

digging an entrance. But nothing came, and perhaps it was just the sand shifting, the earth moving, the rock of the waves pounding against the shore, always, everything, in a state of change.

Aslan had been so fascinated by the universe of the sand grains around him he had not noticed the white sail coming closer and closer to the shore. The sail, it smiled with the warmth of Manu's, filled with the winds that carried her back to him. When she was just an arm's length away, she let down her sails and eased the boat to the coast, hopped out into the water and began to tug it in. He rose to meet her, help her, touch her salt-tinged hair to his lips, pull the rough rope, and the boat was snug on the shore.

By the time they left, the sun had already set. They headed into an orange glow muddied by encroaching darkness. Manu had her face pressed against the glass, was she sleeping, Aslan peeked a look at her, no, her eyes were open and she was staring up into the starry sky. She had been silent for an hour, her legs curled up underneath her as she researched the heavens for an explanation. Where she went, Aslan did not know. If he listened, below the cacophony of the radio, the noise of the car and cars, he could hear her pure and playful humming. It seemed a familiar song, he asked her and she said, "I don't know. I think I made it up," and she turned back to the window, no longer humming; she had been caught.

Eventually, traffic slowed as they came nearer the city, and the hesitation woke Manu from her reflections. She leaned over and kissed his shoulder and Aslan was whole again. She rambled a little about the day and the sailboat, and how many more days she would likely go sailing again before the autumn set in, "It's just too cold in October and I don't have the desire anymore…"

She caught herself in silence again, and turned her sun freckled face to Aslan, asked, "Tell me again, the relationships of atoms?"

"Darling, about what?" Aslan asked, sneaking his hand off the gear shifter to hold hers. They were still an hour from home and a tinge of hunger spread across his stomach, he wondered if he would have the energy yet.

And sensing his hunger pangs, Manu reached into her bag and brought out a snack. She opened the bag for him and fed him so he could keep his eyes on the road. "About the relationships," she said, crumbling up the bag, "When you talk about the lab sometimes, looking at the atoms all day, you talk about them as if they were people. Tell me again."

There are two types of particles that I have observed, the scientist said. There are bosons and fermions.

Bosonic atoms are social. They don't mind having each other around. Whenever there is a potential to trap them, they all accumulate happily in the center. Regard- less of how many of them there are, they gather on top of each other; they do not mind the lack of personal space. They are very good at talking to each other; they are very effective, and collectively show similar behavior. Sometimes you can't even tell one apart from another.

And when you look at them, they seem like one entity even though there are many and many of them. They talk to each other simultaneously and they have strong relationships with one another. And these bosonic atoms, when they come together, because they are so similar seeming, in the end, they don't show a variety of characters. They fail at showing distinct individual identities.

Our examples are photons, which constitutes light, and graviton, which constitutes gravity.

We can say, the scientist added, That they are re- sponsible for enforcing the general orders in the uni- verse because they are social.

And then there are the other kinds of atoms called fermionic atoms. Unlike bosonic atoms, they have strong characters. Once a place is occupied by one of them, the others do not want to be close by. They care about their personal space. You can say, the scientist laughs, they are anti-social.

Because of that, when you put many of them in the same place, depending on how many there are and depending on the place, they end up making very different, complicated structures. As a whole, they are responsible for the variety in our universe.

And those are the reasons why there are so many atoms with different characters.

One snowy evening, Aslan was late coming home from a meeting at the university. He pulled out his phone and called a car. He fiddled for a moment, pinning down his exact location on the digital map, and then marveled at the icon of the car soon approaching his point on the map, turning a corner only a minute a way, driving down the street, turning right, and ah, Aslan looked up to the red SUV stopping in front of him.

Manu was writing at the table when Aslan came home. Dinner was stewing on the stove, and Aslan inhaled dinner and Manu all as one. She peeped up from her notebook, squinted hello, and fell back to her work, re-entering her world to write again, leaving Aslan behind.

The snow fell down outside, big, soft flakes that did not settle on the ground at all, but made everything wet and slippery. Aslan took off his coat and gloves and scarf, his shoes, left it all in the closet by the door and went to the stove to peer into the pot, smell the fragrance again and guess at what she was making. He stirred it once and felt the steam touch his cheeks and burn the cold away.

"It will be ready soon," Manu said, from faraway because she was writing and thinking. When she wrote, Aslan saw in her eyes a distant look as if he was not in the room with him at all, but in a private universe. Her stays were almost always transient, stolen time after work and in between when Aslan came home.

And in the private universe, his Manu became an- other thing. He saw her skin pale and her lips relax, her breathing lengthening out. Sometimes, her eyes would rise from the pages, unseeing, her lips whispering foreign words, perhaps, longing after something as

if forgotten. Then her eyes would brighten and fall back
to the pages.

She seemed to understand the world in a different
reality than he. He tried to imagine it through her eyes as
he stirred the dinner, began to set the plates. She had once
explained it to him, and like an artist, she explained,
"Everything is color and light and rhythm and pattern."

"You see beauty in everything," he told her. "Yes," she
said, "Don't you?"

In her private universe, he would lose her for some
time. She came back when she was ready, but that was
when? She always would look at the clock and say,
"Really, that is how much time has passed?" look at her
pages again. She had control of time, there in her other
place, she was the queen, too slow and to change and to
speed things.

Aslan set the table and brought over the stew, serving
them each and some rice, and he returned to the kitch-
en for the silverware and napkins and glasses. They
began to eat; Aslan fumbled for the remote and played
a show in the background, but between them, they ate
in silence. She was thinking over her story, still, and he
watched her face draw away from herself until she
looked up at him and said, "I'm writing a story about
you, about us..."

Aslan was surprised. "About us?" he asked, eating, half-listening to the noise behind his shoulder. "Would anyone know, that it is us?"

"Oh no," she told him, "It's a story. It won't really be about us. But we will know." She looked down at the notebook beside her arm and fingered the edges. The scientist's wife looked embarrassed, her pale cheeks pink and a red blooming across her brow and neck. "It is the dearest thing I can give you."

Aslan, still perplexed, still not completely understanding, brushed his lips against her cheeks. "Thank you, darling. What is it about?"

"I don't know," she said and he laughed, you don't know. "Not yet. Our story is very young yet."

The scientist, all at once, looked over his wife, and his body filled with warmth and light and love and so much, that all he could do was sit motionless and look at her. He marveled at her capacity to regard the world and imagine and create, taking here and there such things, and making beauty. He sighed.

"Are we flying?" she asked him quietly, looked up to him from her pages. She asked this question to him some times; she was saying her I love yous in the words. "It doesn't feel so long ago that we met, and yet, we've been married two years now... Time with you goes by so fast."

Aslan held his wife in his gaze. "We are flying," he promised.

They fell to eating again. Beneath the noise of the show, outside the wind picked up, howled. They talked about the weather and if it snowed anymore she would work from home the next day, and he would take a day off, if work was canceled, likely to be, the students could not get to their classes.

As talk turned to work and he told her about the upcoming conference he was going to in the spring. They cleaned up and moved to the couch, curled up against each other and listening to the snow howl down outside, settling now in little piles and pockets on the streets.

"Tell me something you are working on now," she asked, pressing her face against his chest, and he sighed, full of love and warmth and light like before, but this time her body was close to him.

Atoms are the best timekeepers, the scientist said. They can keep track of time better than anything we know. We constructed time. If you think about it, time only remarks on change. The passing of seasons, blonde hair turning gray, the rotation of the earth around the sun. Time measures change.

Now, when we measure time, we want something constant. Think of a clock, the pendulum going back and forth, the tick tocks measure time. But even the best mechanical pendulums develop discrepancies.

Atoms keep the most accurate time. When tickled by radio waves, electrons jump back and forth between energy states. A second is 9,192,631,770 cycles of tickling of an atom of cesium jumping back and forth between two energy states.

How does the cesium atomic clock work, my love? Well, the cesium atoms are funneled down a tube where they pass through the radio waves that tickle them.

When the frequency is just right 9,192,631,770 cycles per second then the cesium atoms are tickled and change their energy state.

At the end of the tube, a detector keeps track of the number of atoms that change their energy states. The more finely tuned the radio wave frequency is to 9,192,631,770 cycles per second, the more cesium atoms reach the detector.

The detector reads this information back into the radio wave generator. It synchronizes the frequency of the radio waves with the peak number of cesium atoms striking it. The atomic clock ticks are counted in this frequency. And just as with a single swing of the pendulum, a second is ticked off.

In the spring, Aslan took leave from the university to work on his research. He traveled to Europe for a conference and then met his wife in Istanbul. It was her first time in his country.

They spent some time in the city before moving on towards the Aegean Sea, the Mediterranean. He walked behind his wife as they moved through the cities. Her eyes lighted on everything, she glowed with openness as she sampled dishes in restaurants, always, her spirit curious and forthcoming.

He watched how other eyes fell on her light skin, her blonde hair, her broad smile. How the women stared down at her from second-story windows. Manu was in love and oblivious and Aslan held her hand and held her back from the dangers of passing cars and motorbikes.

She had learned to speak, a little and not very well, but her determination to conquer the language touched his soul. In the early days, they had lain in bed pouring over a textbook, and laughing, she teased out bizarre sentences, learned tricky suffixes. She had wanted to learn the moment she met him, asking him the night after as they ate breakfast of eggs together, "And how do you count to ten?" In a week, she had counted for him.

Still, Manu could not be infinitely elastic. As their travel deepened into the heart of Turkey, he felt her tense when approached and asked. She had given up playfully responding to him in his language, and instead yawned out English.

Even Manu was not so malleable and the food and the weather weighed down on her, yes, it was too much even for her, and she grew impatient waiting for Aslan to order her food.

"Where are you going?" he asked her. They had just returned to their hotel in Ankara and it was the sunlight fading into stars.

"I would like to go for a walk," Manu said tersely. Her face was strained and her eyes were dull. Aslan knew, her soul was clawing her apart. Her chaos and inability to restore balance pained her even more as she tried to please Aslan with smiles, with her promise to forever be open. Manu's sadness agitated Aslan as all he wanted to do was fix and resolve and placate her into peace and smiles. But her sadness welled into despair, and she withdrew from him, fell into silences, sought her interior world, secreting away from Aslan and out of his grasp.

He watched her go, and whispered, as the door closed, "Be careful, aşkım." Time apart from Manu, even moments, darkened his thoughts. She was a wanderer, always wandering from place to place, leaving him for a few weeks to sail in France with her uncle, always packing her bags and kissing him on cheek, "But I like to go. I like to miss you and come back to you". Her teasing smile bit his heart each time she stepped into a taxi.

Aslan rose from the bed and lurked around their room until he settled down on the balcony. It was a warm, clear evening and from the streets came a sea of voices, washing over him and blending into the night noises, the whisper of a faint breeze. He looked down at his watch, then to the streets below him, hoping to catch a glimpse of blonde in a sea so dark.

He would say he was sorry when she returned. He would grab her by the waist and tell her his love of her. Manu, lovely Manu was never disagreeable. Occasionally an obscure emotion would cross over her brow, and she would fall into sullenness unlike her, disappearing at odd hours for solitude, for silences. He looked at his watch again, knowing in his heart she had not turned against him, but to see her lost and drowning tore his soul. He had never known the feeling before he met Manu, and watching her cry one night, uncertain of herself, he had brought her into his arms not knowing what else to do. She was so beautiful when she cried.

His ears pricked to hear a sound, but it was not Manu at the door. When they had only began dating, he had turned to her, unsure and feeling so much for her and so afraid of the richness of love, the promise of pain, he stroked her cheek and said, "Will we ever get bored of knowing one another?" Manu, so beautiful and wise, looked at with clear and knowing eyes and said, "We will never fully know one another."

The scientist told his wife the story about entangled atoms. It was her favorite story.

The rules of quantum physics state, he reminded her, that an unobserved photon exists in all possible states simultaneously, however, when observed or measured, exhibits only one state. And, he added, remember that spin is depicted as an axis of rotation. But actual particles do not rotate.

Entanglement occurs when a pair of particles, such as photons, interacts physically. If I take a laser beam in the lab and fire it through a certain type of crystal, this can cause individual photons to be split into pairs of entangled photons. And large distances can separate these photons, hundreds of miles. Possibly even more.

There is a photon in Somerville, and it begins its rotation in an up-spin state. An entangled photon in Izmir, far away, takes up a state similar to the photon in Somerville; however, its rotation is a down-spin state. The transfer of state between our photon in Somerville and our photon in Izmir takes place at a speed of at least 10,000 times the speed of light, potentially even instantaneously, regardless of the distance.

Can you imagine, my darling, the possibilities? It is, as Einstein once said, "Spooky action at a distance." The scientist paused, and then asked, "Have I ever explained why entangled atoms feel the same thing? Because they are one. They are not two anymore."

"Has the sun set? Is it time?" The wife of a friend asked, reaching for a date. Her husband nodded, "Yes, it's time," and everyone began to eat. Aslan looked around the table at his friends assembled. They began talking about jobs and visas, and they recommended each to each this person and that person to see, "Let me send you their information," one said to another as they served themselves salad or reached for the bread.

He watched Manu listen, too, as the language changed in and out, and sometimes Aslan would touch her knee secretly under the table or serve her something more. They were all Aslan's friends, and though, becoming Manu's, still his wife was almost too polite in collecting the dishware after, helping the friend's wife in the kitchen, too quiet as she sat down amongst the others and listened. He touched her knee as she leaned her head into his shoulder, and though he would have liked to stay more, hear the raucous conversation of one friend to them all, he knew his wife was tired and she would never say a thing at all to draw him away too soon from his friends.

They left the living room of familiar faces and took a taxi home. Manu tucked her head into Aslan's body, her voice faint and dreamy as she answered his questions. The taxi lights broke through the night, and soon they were home.

But in the elevator, she suddenly came alive and warm in his arms as they kissed, and she smiled, falling away from his hands, and then with wide-awake eyes, into his body.

He knew her body well, her smells, her tender points, her shivers. Her familiarity exhilarated him, coming to him vibrant and open and his. She whispered in his ear, I want to be entangled, before both of them gave away, falling deeply into one another, closer and closer and never close enough.

As they lay in bed, now, looking at one another and talking about all the things on their mind, gossiping a little bit about their friends, sometimes murmuring on the future, Aslan thought again of his friends at the table that night, all around the table, their movements and actions, the way they ate and the way they talked. He thought, None of them know how much I love her. He brought her closer to him and pinched her cheeks and kissed her forehead, None of them know her as I do, her infinite secret treasures.

"Tell me again what you thought when we first met? I want to hear you tell me again."

"I recognized you," she breathed into his ear.

He thought of their friends at the table, thought again of the husbands and wives, the single friends, the dating friends. He thought of all the love in the world and his love for Manu, and as her eyelids heavied, he asked her, "Did I ever tell you about the lives of atoms?"

In the lab, the scientist said, I change the states of atoms. I try to get them to come together. Sometimes the frequencies aren't right and they come together, collide, go running off in different directions, disappearing. Sometimes they come together for a moment and I think, "Ah, the two have found love," but then they argue and come apart.

In order for two atoms to realize their strongest bond, their characters should match. And when I say this, I don't mean that they should be the same. One of them should be the giver. The other one should be the taker. One of them gives their electrons to the other one. And when that amount of giving and taking matches, that's when the strongest possible bond between atoms happens.

Their characters, when I said characters earlier, their characters are defined by how many electrons they have. Atoms have a nucleus and a certain number of electrons. And they always want a complete shell of electrons around the nucleus. Sometimes two atoms are not complete until they come together.

There is a group of atoms, their shell is already complete by electrons. They don't want to give or take either. They don't make any bonds with any other atoms. They are called noble gases.

When the atoms form bonds together and form molecules, they lose their characters and they become something else together.

The most profound example is water. Water is formed by hydrogen and oxygen. Oxygen is easily flammable. And hydrogen burns. But when these two come together, they form something that will quell a fire.

Summer in Boston always came slowly, winter seeping into spring, spring a miserable mix of hopelessness and false promises. And then suddenly, Aslan would open his eyes and feel the sun on his face and he would leave the balcony door open to let in the breezes. He rose from the couch now and crossed the living room to step out onto the balcony. The sun was setting and the city in the distance glowed gold.

Manu was sitting on the couch, a great blanket spread out over her body. With her nimble fingers, she drove a threaded needle in and out through the fabric, stitching together myriad of pieces. At first, when she began four months ago, he did not understand the pattern she was making, the reason she chose each specific color. Little by little, a design appeared. Manu's head lifted and she murmured to Aslan on the balcony, "I think I will be finished in a few more months. Hopefully just before," and she lowered her head, returned to stitching.

The next morning, they rose together, blessed by the luxury of the weekend. As customary, they went to the bathroom to shower. Aslan first washed his hair and beard while Manu waited. She would reach above him and collect some water on her hands, washed her face until he was finished. He stepped aside, then, to let the water fall onto her skin, lathering soap in his hands.

Then Aslan washed his wife.

Aslan had washed his wife perhaps from the day of their first shower together. He was filled with pleasure to feel the curves of her body with his soapy hands, to reach into all her crevices, to touch her feet. She became all her parts: a hand, a nose, a breast. All of her familiar, warm, and kind.

But in the recent months, Manu's body had begun to change. Her malleability always amazed him. Her skin seemed to glow and her hair grew thicker, lightened, too. Her eyes spoke of a secret he longed to know. She blinked, and they promised to tell him soon.

Her soul underwent the greatest transformation; it was the secret her eyes wanted to tell him. He found her humming more often, dreamily looking down at her hands as they caressed her body. She was thinking, thinking of a future.

And how that future made her suffer. He heard her in the bathroom sometimes in the morning, coughing and groaning. He would prepare a meal and she would cover her mouth, shake her head no. She dozed more on the couch after work, unable to wait for him to come home.

Aslan finished washing his wife, let her pass so she could rinse off the soap. She closed her eyes and tilt- ed her head back, her mouth slightly open. He could not believe it, her changes and her flexibility. He could not understand, and knew he could never comprehend her awareness. He had known her so fully for so many years, had become as much a part of her as she had of him, and yet this change in her stunned him.

As he made breakfast for the both of them, Manu began again at her quilt. "I see now what you are designing," Aslan said, making the eggs, "You tell our story so well."

"You think so," Manu said vaguely, ever timid.

He set the eggs out on a plate, grabbed two forks and brought it over to the table. Manu let the quilt go and

joined him. She reached for a piece of toast. He listened
to their silences for a while, and then cleared his throat to
say, "I don't think I ever told you how atoms are created."

It is amazing to think sometimes, the scientist began,
looking over her quilt, how over four billion years ago,
at the start of biological evolution, we started with the
most basic elements. All organisms are made of essen-
tially the same material. You and I and that quilt, the
plants that line our windowsill. In our world, we are
all the same. Consider it like the alphabet. Individually
we have letters, but together, we have words, and even
more complex, sentences, punctuation and grammar.

Then we have the paragraph, the short story, the novel.

The scientist paused and said, But I'm getting ahead of
myself because I wanted to tell you how atoms are created.

In the beginning, both space and time were created
in the Big Bang. This happened over 13.7 billion years
ago. Afterwards, the universe was a very hot, forever
expanding soup of fundamental particles. The universe
expanded quickly in those first moments. It is still
expanding, but now at a more or less constant rate. And
as it grows, it cools.

At first, the universe was only radiation. But soon quarks combined to form baryons, or protons and neutrons. When the universe was only three minutes old, it had cooled enough for these protons and neutrons to form nuclei. We began to have elements like hydrogen, helium, lithium, and beryllium. The first letters of the universe.

Still, the universe was far too hot to let these nuclei attract electrons and form atoms. Three hundred thousand years later, the universe was cool enough for atoms to exist. With right conditions and force, these four elements: hydrogen, helium, lithium, and beryllium, combined and shifted, and changed until the universe had eighty-eight natural elements.

The story of how those eighty-eight came about are for another time, darling. It's getting late. But look at your quilt. The patch of blue here or the red-striped. It is not the pieces that make it compelling, but when it is finished, its completeness.

And so, my love, beauty is not in the unseen things that make you, but the way those unseen things are you.

From the other room, Aslan heard Manu cooing and

playing with the child. Yildiz's laughter now and then pierced his thoughts, distracting his fingers. He put down the clarinet and rejoined his family in the bedroom.

Manu was on the floor next to their bed, watching as Yildiz pushed with her pudgy arms off from the quilt. The child crouched for a moment, looking at her mother. She had the same blue eyes as Manu, though her coloring was darker. A wild pouf of black hair, "she looks more like you," Manu would say. Their daughter fought to stand up, stood for a moment with the mild astonishment, before taking a step and falling. She looked up at her mother's face to understand her reaction. Manu laughed and clapped. The baby grunted, laughed again.

Over and over, Manu cheered Yildiz to take a step towards her. Aslan watched from the bed, hovering over both of them, too far for the child to reach out to.

From where he sat, Aslan could smell Manu. Her scent had always been evocative; from the first night he met her in the restaurant. She smelled of vanilla and a heavier, muskier scent that reminded him of his childhood, going into the park with his parents and sister, drinking tea at the table in the summer evenings. It was a dark golden smell; it was all over her and in her clothes and pores. And there was mint, suddenly, light and clear and poignant. An aroma of milk, warm and internal. He could smell all of this, lying inches from her. She knew he loved her scent and every time she traveled, left a vial of her perfume to keep on him while she was away.

It was over two years ago that he and Manu had sat down to eat dinner one night after work. His wife had been talking about a friend who was having difficulty conceiving and he asked naively, "What if you can't have children?" Manu did not answer. The thought, perhaps, had never occurred to her, and she said nothing, looking down at her plate. "I would be so sad," she told him finally, her thoughts turning more and more away from him and into her secret, internal world. He touched her hand, "No, don't be sad, aşkım."

That night, Manu had fallen asleep quickly and easily, wrapped along Aslan's side. But he was thinking of the conversation earlier. Outside he heard the train rattle by, the cars coin up over the hill. The idea of children had never appealed to him, but it did not repulse him either. They were their own distant things and he was his own, and they had never interacted much in the past. Even with his friends' children, they played amongst themselves or with their favorite amclar while he sat drinking tea and eating the desserts. How could Manu want such things, knowing the sacrifices and consequences, the pain? Why was she so impervious and unafraid of pain?

And then Yildiz had come into their lives. Their star, Yildiz, whose laughter was such a beautiful song greeting every day. Whose cries brought Aslan terrible sorrow and discomfort as he rocked her back and forth, tormented by her scrunched, red face. He would sing to her, anything to calm her.

Manu sat up and kissed Aslan, leaving him with their daughter. He heard her move around in the kitchen, metal singing, the rounded sound of water filling a pot. Yildiz crawled over to the bed and raised herself up to reach her baba. Aslan collected her in his arms and lay on the bed with her.

He loved the way she smelled. Of newness, clean and soft. He sniffed her thick hair, fragrant with life. She smelled of baby smells, of the sickly smell of spit-up on her shirt, of milk, of sweaty hands. He kissed her to him, then let her crawl all over him, let her pull at his beard and mustache. He let her babble, asking her baby philosophy in her baby language. "Yes," he would answer and she would respond in grunts and cooing, "Yes, that's right…"

They lay together, listening to Manu cooking dinner

in the kitchen, faraway. As he listened, he turned to Yildiz and said to her, "I don't know how, but your sweetness has doubled." The baby burbled, and he wiped the spit from her cheek. "Come, my little one," he said, pulling her into his lap.

You would not think it is possible that your sweetness could double, the scientist said, because your sweetness is already infinite. But I promise you that it can.

The real numbers between one and two are infinite, don't you agree? Well, let us suppose that we then take a measure between one and three. It is then doubled. And so we must count every real number between one and three. That is how your infinite sweetness is doubled.

From room to room, he heard their whispers and quiet voices, the sudden peal of Yildiz's laughter ringing out and echoing against the high ceilings. Aslan watched his wife and child from the corner of his eye, from the other room, always aslant. He liked to see her bend down towards the girl, say something in her ear, point to the colors, the blends of textures, telling little stories about the artist, about the painting, and Yildiz's eyes twinkled in delight, her rosebud mouth just open and breathless. Yildiz was as her mother, an artist in spirit.

The family moved from one room to another, and Aslan dawdled behind them, trying to grasp after the images his wife and daughter fluttered to in earnest. Perhaps they exhausted the beauty and meaning by the time Aslan peered at the vocabulary of color. Manu had once said, "When I see this painting," and she had gestured to a garden of Monet, "It is like electricity through my body. I physically shiver."

She had said that sometime when they had first dated. It had been her idea to come to the museum, "There is an exhibit," she told him with bright eyes, the constellations on fire, "I want to show you something." Manu tantalized him that night, taking him a long way through the galleries, climbing up the white marble stairs and pointing to the ceiling murals, "Do you know the stories of the gods?" and before he could answer, she told him every story, her fingers dancing mario-nettes spreading wide the mythology. Aslan was quiet, basking in the glow of her fire, her burning eyes.

Manu had led him through the museum slowly, slowly approaching the gallery she wanted to take him to because she liked the thrill of delay. He followed her. They had had six dates before and this was their seventh night, and each time their presence merged together, some fabric of their soul intertwined a little more. Each felt this, quietly acknowledging the secret with lowered eyes as he took her hand and she led him through the galleries.

Aslan watched the ghosts of their youths be replaced by Manu's fine figure, the smaller figure of Yildiz. She had her mother's eyes, spirit, artistic urge. She was both light and dark. Some days, the tilt of her head would remind him of his sister when she was young. Another day, he would ask Yildiz to do something, and she would say, No! boldly in declaration, No! just like her mother.

Their voices were absorbed in the ancient world galleries. Manu told the stories of the myths. Aslan point- ed to artifacts and said to Yildiz, "And this comes from my hometown…" "…and this comes from not far from where my parents now live…" Yildiz stood on her toes to peer into the glass cases, her young mind uncomprehending the significance of time and human history.

"When will we go see Babaanne and Dede?"

"Soon, tatlım," Aslan said, brushing her hair.

Yildiz went from glass case to glass case, reading the

plaques and asking questions. "It is iron, it is all made
of iron," she said.

"Yes," he said, lifting her up and carrying her. The
museum was closing and they moved towards the exit
together. Yildiz rested her head on his shoulder, the
weight of the day's adventure falling over her. "Do you
know the story of iron?" The girl shook her head. "It is
a very special story. It is why your mother's ring is made
from iron. You could say," he kissed the girls cheek,
"Iron is created in the heart of a star."

The story of iron, began the scientist, begins in the
center of a red giant star. Red giants are a hundred
times bigger than our sun. They have many layers, just
like people do, a layer of helium, of carbon, of hydrogen.
You have to peel away each layer to get to its core. The
red giant stars will change all of its helium into carbon
and oxygen, and then it decides to change the carbon
and oxygen into iron atoms. The red giants are always
changing, they can never stay still.

Iron is the heaviest atom the star can make, and
when all of its carbon and oxygen is turned into iron in
its heart, the star becomes a supernova and explodes.

Can you imagine, tatlım, when a supernova explodes? First it shoots out all its carbon, oxygen, and iron atoms far and wide across the Universe. It makes a real big mess. And eventually, gravity pulls these atoms into new planets, like Earth. All of the iron on Earth was originally inside of stars.

Earth's heart is mostly made of molten iron. The ground contains iron, and so do the plants and the flowers and the trees. So do you and me. Remember, iron came from the heart of stars.

And that's why you saw in the museum, the tools and the jewelry and the art made of iron. Long ago, people started to use iron to build and make things. The learned that iron was useful to make weapons, and so they fought wars. Remember, iron came from the heart of stars.

And that is why, tatlım, the scientist said, tucking his sleeping daughter into the car, when I asked your mother for her love I gave her a ring made from a star.

She met him at the entrance, almost as she did thirty years ago. Aslan did not recall that night well, though, but Manu would always say, "When I saw you, I recognized you." She stood waiting for him, her coat draped over her arm, wearing an elegant long wool skirt. Her cheeks were flushed, so she must not have been waiting for him long.

Manu rushed to kiss him. All their lives, Manu has always rushed to kiss him, drawing his face towards her with both hands, as if they had been apart for years. She gave each kiss a renewed significance. Her love was warm as it moved through her lips, moving gold through Aslan's body.

A waiter took them to a table in the back, set down the menus, asked what they would like to drink. For a moment, Aslan felt uncomfortable sensation, certain awkwardness. They stuttered, they paused. It was like they were on their first date. Manu would not say happy anniversary, not directly. She was more subdued, indirect, as at their wedding, her white dress so simple and made of linen, she didn't care.

Yildiz had called them each that day from France. Why did she have to go so far away? Sometimes Aslan would look at the photos she sent him along her travels and wonder at how tall, at how beautiful she had become. So like her mother. Though dark like him.

The girl, but no, she was a young woman now, had her mother's light blue eyes and pale skin, his dark hair.

And her voice, too, when she had called in the afternoon, he had for a moment mistaken, became confused and called her Manu. "Ah, Baba, no, it's Yildiz" and she giggled, faraway, her laughter caught in a box through time.

The waiter came back with the tapas and they began to eat. The pauses were familiar and tranquil, they remembered each other, and every now and then he looked up at her, studied the gray in her hair, the wrinkles by the corners of her eyes.

"How did this happen?" Manu asked suddenly, a wink and a smile as she took another bite. She had been asking him for thirty years.

"You don't remember the story?" He asked, still amused by their game.

"No, I don't, remind me."

Aslan drank and said, "You were eating here, alone, and I approached you."

"I was just eating?" Through narrowed eyes she asked, her voice tempting him to play.

"No, you were reading a book."

"And you approached me and we started talking? No, I think I rebuffed you a few times."

"Why did you start talking to me?"

"You wouldn't leave me alone to finish my book, so I

thought, 'Well, why not?'" Her eyes splintered into a million pieces of laughter. Aslan reached out and pinched her cheeks.

"And what were you reading?" "Invisible Cities."

How had they met, a boy from a village in Turkey, a girl from a village in Pennsylvania. How had they met, how did they have a life together, and was it as good and as lovely as they thought it would be in the beginning?

They were walking home now, arm in arm against the cold. She leaned into his shoulder a little fatigued. Her body through the coat was frail and thin. They arrived at their apartment and went then to their routine of married life, Manu snuck up to Aslan on the couch with a wrapped box in hand, "I have something for you."

Aslan unfolded the tissue paper and revealed a hardbound book. The cover read, The Lives of Atoms. "Manu, what is this?"

And she told him, told him all, all the secrets he had wanted to know all along. "Do you remember when I told you I was writing a story about us?" She held the book out to him. "Aşkım..."

He knew her face, knew her tears so well, knew the curves of her body, the scars, the freckled birthmark. And knowing her gave him so much pleasure that he pushed all the more against her to be as close as he could ever be. When he had wrapped his arms around her to sleep side by side as they had for so many years, Manu whispered, "Are you real?"

He kissed her neck, "Only as real as you are."

Long after Manu had drifted off, still, Aslan could not sleep. An impulse stirred inside of him and disrupted his thoughts. He rose from bed and went into the kitchen for a drink, and while looking over the room towards the view of Boston; he saw the book Manu had given him. The book was finely printed, simple and elegant. He read the inscription, turned a few pages here and there, reading into glimpses of memories. He turned a page towards the back and began to read:

When the nuclei of radioactive atoms are unstable, they break down and change into completely different types of atoms. This is called radioactive decay. No one can predict when an individual atom might decay.

When an unstable nucleus decays, there are three ways that it will go about it. Its nucleus may give out an alpha particle, which are two protons and new neutrons. Or, it may give out a beta particle, which is a fast-moving electron. Or, it may give out a gamma ray.

Sometimes, the nuclear radiation ionizes materials. This happens when particles lose electrons and become positively charged, or when particles gain electrons and become negatively charged. Ionization can be harmful to living cells. Alpha particles are good ionizers because they have larger mass and a greater charge.

Returning to half-lives, I have one more thought. You never know when an atom will decay, but that doesn't mean it is completely random. It is the same thing as the expectancy of human life. One never knows when a person will die, but there is an average for when a person will die. For example, an average person lives about seventy years, and in a similar way, a half-life can be determined. A half-life is measured half from many atoms together, say a million, and one counts the time when half the atoms are dead. So, when that time happens, the clock is stopped and the time of the half-life of an atom is defined.

Yildiz helped Aslan into the chair. She was a woman now, her long, dark hair plaited over her shoulder, she was a darker version of Manu from a long time ago.

Her voice was even the same so that at times when she called him, he would say, "Manu, Manu?" and Yildiz would have to remind him. And again, his heart was empty and lost.

She sat across from him and asked him if needed anything. He told her he didn't want anything, but still, she got up to make tea and brought it back to him. She brought the faded quilt from the bed and wrapped it around his shoulders. Yildiz was always fiddling with her hands, taming something. He thought it was just her, but he remembered once when his spirit was also agitated. Now, Aslan felt as if he was freed from the impatience he had felt all his life. Looking over the unlined face of his daughter, he thought, "Perhaps only the young."

Yildiz was not so young, though. She had a career and two young children. She was both scientist and artist, and her complexity often mystified Aslan until he thought of her mother. Yildiz was part her father and part her mother. She was a collage of Aslan's darkness, Manu's lightness.

Yet, she was entirely her own being. Looking at her, he wondered if at an atomic level, she carried the memories of Manu and him, previous generations. His daughter asked how he was, how he was feeling.

He felt like a burden on her time; she came often, and how did she manage with the children and work as a scientist and artist? He gazed at his daughter as she prattled on in her sweet voice. How beautiful she was. How proud he was of her.

He noticed the ring on her hand as she held the tea mug. It was made of iron. Manu had been a slow burning giant. A red star. No matter how far the distance, she was always seen within the universe.

He asked her if she remembered the story of iron and she answered in their language, "Yes, Baba," a little roll of her eyes. She has heard his story a hundred times before, but after reconciling her impatience, she then asked Aslan, "But, please, Baba, tell me once more..." Because once more may be never more, he heard it in her tone.

They look at each other and he told the story again. After the hour, Yildiz's husband came by with the children. He was tall and from Iran. This always disappointed Aslan; wherever the husband would have been from would have always disappointed Aslan. His daughter was his universe.

The children, a boy and a girl ran towards Aslan with hands opened, begging, "Dede, Dede..." The girl was named Merve. She had neither Yildiz's features nor her husband's. Instead, her hair was light and her skin was pale and freckled. Her eyes were blue with flecks of gold, like a universe. She was older and heavier, but Aslan pulled her into his lap.

The boy was younger. His name was Metin. Yildiz said he looked like Aslan when he was little; she had looked at his pictures. Perhaps he did. His big brown eyes and pouf of hair. Aslan was happy at least to see the images of his family in the children, and only glimmers and suggestions of Yildiz's husband.

The children were never impatient with him like Yildiz. They sat in his lap and listened. They were never hurried to go anywhere. He thought of when Yildiz was an infant and his discomfort with her fragile figure, her plaintive cries that set him on edge. Her children, even when they were babies, had never annoyed him. He had found new joy in their tiny movements, their feeble attempts to win his love.

The children broke his thoughts with a whimper. "Tell us a story, Dede…" Aslan looked to Yildiz for cues, and seeing her frown, then soften, he nodded and turned towards the children. "Have I ever told you about atoms and death?"

I want to tell you another story first. Have you been able to pick out Orion's stars in the sky? Have you noticed the red star that marks the hunter's left shoulder? Betelgeuse is a red giant soon running out of fuel.

Stars, like our Sun, generate energy through nuclear fusion reactions. The heart of a star is dense and hot, turning hydrogen into helium, releasing this energy and making the star shine.

Few things are infinite, and eventually the hydrogen in the core will get used up, and the star will end up with a heart of helium. Fusion will slow as energy no longer flows out of the core, and gravity, the force that originally created the star, will squeeze its core so tight that it will start to heat up. It begins to swell to 100 times its former size, to what we now call a red giant. When there is no more hydrogen, the star begins to fuse helium, and the helium turns to carbon. The star lives a bit longer, fusing carbon to oxygen, and then iron. But iron fusion, instead of giving out energy, takes it in. And our supermassive star collapses and explodes.

And when the red giants explode, they force new elements that they created within themselves out into the Universe. This includes the carbon in your teeth,

the oxygen we breathe. The iron in your mother's –
your grandmother's – ring. We are all made from the
stuff of stars.

Now I will tell you about the death of atoms, the
scientist began his story. Particles are not living things,
remember. They cannot die. They exist in a continuous
present with neither past nor future. They will regroup
to new states, but they do not transfer memories, only
their presence.

The story of death should be told, the scientist
continued, We are the most rare of the species in that
we are forever aware of our own mortality and fragility.
But the story of death does not always have to be so
unpleasant. I am telling you this story, my loved ones,
to prepare you for the life ahead of you.

What happens to those atoms in our body when we
die? They end up all over the place. Once the process of
decomposition begins, the array of molecules in our
body – from fats to DNA – are broken down. Their
atoms are transformed into new molecules. Your carbon
atoms may be found in a bacterium cell wall, or com-
bine with oxygen and be released on the breath of a
butterfly.

Our atoms, which were borrowed all along, return to
other organisms and materials, again and again, trans-

forming and changing, carrying on atoms that billions
and billions of years ago were born in the bellies of stars.

About the Author

Lee Okan is a writer based in Boston. She is currently doing her PhD in Creative Writing at Aberystwyth University in Wales. The Lives of Atoms is her first novel.

Nixes Mate Books features small-batch artisanal literature, created by writers that use all 26 letters of the alphabet and then some, honing their craft the time-honored way: one line at a time.

Other or Forthcoming Nixes Mate titles: